SIMON FRUELUN

Translated by K.E. Semmel

MILK

AND OTHER STORIES

Santa Fe Writers Project

www.sfwp.com
www.simonfruelund.com

Simon Fruelund is the author of five books, among them *Borgerligt tusmørke* (2006)—published as *Civil Twilight* by Spout Hill Press in 2013—Verden og Varvara (The World and Varvara, 2010), and *Panamericana* (2012).

The characters and events portrayed in this book are fictitious. Any similarity to real persons, living or dead, is coincidental and not intended by the author.

Copyright © 1997 by Simon Fruelund
Translation copyright © 2013 K.E. Semmel
First published in Danish as *Mælk: Noveller* 1997 by Gyldendal

Library of Congress Cataloging-in-Publication Data

Fruelund, Simon, 1966-
 [Short stories. Selections. English]
 Milk & other stories / Simon Fruelund.
    pages cm
 Translated from Danish.
 ISBN 978-0-9882252-7-5
 1. Fruelund, Simon, 1966—Translations into English. I. Title. II. Title: Milk and
    other stories.
 PT8177.16.R84M3413 2013
 839.81'38—dc23
                                2013001290

Published by SFWP
369 Montezuma Ave. #350
Santa Fe, NM 87501
www.sfwp.com

Made available in part by a grant from:

STATENS
KUNSTRÅD
DANISH ARTS COUNCIL

Table of Contents

Tide

It was early spring. I walked past the inn and saw a young couple stepping out of a silver-gray Peugeot. They had driven over while the water was rising, and the car was wet along the sides. Each had shoulder-length hair and was of slender build. The man was just a little taller than the woman and they resembled each other like two siblings.

That same evening the innkeeper, Poul, called.

—There's a couple who'd like to go out tomorrow.

I looked at the tide table and gave him a time. Then I went out to the barn to get the wagon ready. I swept it out and arranged a row of straw bales along each of its sides. I checked the oil in the tractor and filled it up with diesel. Before I went inside again, I glanced toward the sky. There was a thin cloud cover, and almost no wind. It'll be nice out tomorrow, I thought.

The next morning I woke to the sound of raindrops on the window. I put water on for coffee and went out to check on the sheep. When I returned, the window in the kitchen was all fogged up. I ate breakfast and watched the rain through a small opening, which I kept wiping clear with my shirtsleeve.

Five minutes before ten I started the tractor and drove to the inn. The young couple sat in a corner of the dining room eating breakfast.

—They know it costs extra when there's only two? I said to the innkeeper, who stood behind the counter.

He nodded.

—And there's no guarantee they'll see anything, I said.

—That's fine.

He walked over and exchanged a few words with them, and they raised their heads and turned to me. The young man nodded almost imperceptibly, and the woman registered my presence like someone who sees a ship far away. Then she dipped her head and said something to the man.

The innkeeper returned.

—They'll be ready in five minutes.

I nodded at him and went out to the parking lot. It was still raining, and I seated myself in the tractor cab.

Fifteen minutes later the door opened.

They had each borrowed rain gear from the innkeeper, I noticed. Their pant legs bunched at their feet, and their sleeves covered their hands. The woman wore a pair of sturdy insulated boots, the man a pair of green rubber boots.

I climbed from the tractor to help them up. We walked to the back of the wagon, and I opened the tailgate.

—It might get a little cold, I said.

—We have extra clothes, the man said and nodded in the direction of a little backpack the woman held in her hand.

We drove through town and onto the dike. The water had begun to retreat and small islands of sand poked up everywhere. With the tractor crawling down the dike, I cast a glance in each of the mirrors: in one I could see him, in the other her. I could see him smiling and saying something to her; I could see her staring ahead of us, past the mirror and out across the water.

It was the first time I was out that year, and the fall storms had dug new ruts in the sand and filled up old ones. One spot was so deep I had to drive around it to get past. The rain lessened, and a short while later I noticed that the young couple had pulled their hoods down.

She got out a camera and I watched her photograph a flock of starlings that passed us.

When we were almost halfway out, I noticed something lying on a sandbank to our right. I veered off route, and when we got a bit closer, I was able to see that it was a sailboard: its orange sail swelling off and on in the weak breeze. I climbed from the tractor, and as I bent over the board, I realized that the woman was standing right beside me. She stared at it, and then turned and snapped a picture of the tractor and wagon.

I noted the spot, and we went on.

The water level had now fallen so low that you could see lugworm burrows on the sand. In certain spots the water looked like nothing more than dark stains.

We reached the breeding ground, cordoned off with orange tape, before we saw the first seal. It lay with its hind flippers in the air and its head on the sand.

We continued along the demarcation, and soon a small group of seals followed us in the water. At the end of the breeding ground, I halted the tractor and the young couple jumped from the wagon. I climbed out and watched them head toward the water's edge. The seals kept their distance, but the youngest of them swam in circles toward the shore: suddenly it appeared just fifteen feet from land. The woman squatted down and extended her hand.

For a moment the seal stood still, water dripping from its white whiskers and onto its spotted coat. Then it thrust itself sideways and swam off in a half-circle. The man eased the camera from the woman and stood poised for the next time the seal turned up.

The other seals grew more courageous and swam toward the shore. A pair raised their heads right near the beach; the man photographed them, and the woman squatted and talked to them.

After a little while the seals retreated, and the young couple watched them go. The woman had risen and was now resting her head on his shoulder. Then they turned and walked up to me.

The woman smiled.

—How much time is there? the man asked.

I looked across the water.

—A little less than an hour, I said.

They walked back to the water's edge. They followed it a ways and then angled up over the sandbank. I seated myself in the tractor cab to eat from my lunch box, and when I looked for them again they were gone.

I watched for them now and again.

After an hour, I still couldn't see them. Wind had begun to blow from the west, and because the tide could change at any moment, I started the tractor and began driving slowly forward.

I followed their footprints until I reached the place where they'd gone over the sandbank. Then I honked the tractor's horn.

I looked back the way I'd come. Already water was filling in the wheel tracks.

I honked the horn a few times.

I climbed from the tractor and called after them.

—Hello, I yelled. I didn't know their names.

After fifteen minutes, I caught a glimpse of two tiny figures walking toward me from far away.

I drove to meet them, and as I drew the tractor up beside them, they smiled as if nothing was wrong. I told them they were late.

—It's so easy to forget about time out here, the man said, helping the woman up on the wagon. They sat close to each other on the left side. Now the water was seriously beginning to rise, and I drove back as fast as I could. Water sprayed from the tractor's rear wheels, and the young couple scooted toward the center of the wagon. In the mirror I could see them huddled together. When we were only halfway in, we drove through a foot of water. When the island became visible, the water had risen almost two feet.

I gripped the steering wheel hard and felt the sweat form on my stomach.

Only when we arrived on the dike did I have time to glance in the mirror again. The man and woman sat in the same position. It didn't look as though they were talking. They sat as if they were hypnotized and stared in the same direction, toward the sea.

When we pulled up in front of the inn, it had begun to rain again. The man handed me the agreed-upon payment, and they hurried in. That's when I noticed sand on the woman's rain jacket.

I stood a bit under the awning before I followed them inside. I opened the glass door and saw the innkeeper sitting at a table doing his books. I sat opposite him and waited for him to look up.

—Any seals? he said

—Yeah.

He added a column of figures and raised his head.

His eyes rested heavily on me as I told him about the sailboard. He put the pencil down on the table.

After I had described the board pretty closely, he got to his feet without saying a word and went into the kitchen.

I heard him talk on the telephone, and then I heard his wife begin to cry, at first softly, then louder. I remained seated at the table.

In a little while the innkeeper returned.

—Let me know if there's anything I can do, I said.

He shook his head and followed me to the door.

—I don't think so, he said.

When I came home, I couldn't relax. I thought about the young couple and the innkeeper's son, and then I thought about Karen. I searched for my pipe, and when I couldn't find it, I went out to the sheep. Rain drummed on the roof, and in a short while I heard the helicopter. One of the sheep came forward and licked my hand.

They act like they have all the time in the world, I thought.

What Is It?

Jakob is my son from my second marriage. He must have heard me arrive, because as I backed the van up to his building, there he stood suddenly beside me. He looked smaller, younger; maybe it was the sneakers he wore and the loose-fitting T-shirt. He lifted his hand and made a 90-degree angle with his thumb and index finger, the kind of thing truck drivers do as they pass each other. Typical Jakob, I thought. When things seem their worst, he always has a gesture or a story to make you smile. I smiled and found the emergency brake, near the rear left side of the wheel, halfway to the pedals.

I got out of the car and we hugged.

—What a mess, I said.

—Yeah, he said, grimacing.

We stood looking at each other for a moment.

—C'mon, he said.

We went through the entrance and into the front hallway. Their apartment was on the ground floor, and the door was wide open.

—Everything's in here, he said, and I followed him into the bedroom. I recognized the heavy mahogany desk that had once belonged to my father. Around it were about twenty-five boxes stacked three or four levels high, and beside them: a light blue mattress, a stereo system, a TV, and a white wardrobe. I tried to picture it all in the van.

—We'll manage, I said. We'll make it fit.

—Helene will be back in about an hour, he said. Let's try to be out of here by then.

It was as if he stared at my right ear as he said it. I nodded—I couldn't do anything else—and brought my hand up to my ear, then rubbed my earlobe between my fingers.

We took the boxes first. One box, with medical books inside, was extremely heavy and we had to haul it out together. Otherwise we grabbed one each; he trotted, and I tried to keep up. It was autumn, the air crisp and clear, but before long I could feel the sweat trickling down my arms. My heart thumped so hard in my chest that I was forced to stop. After I'd carried out five boxes, I slowed my pace, and managed to carry out four more. Jakob got the rest.

—Could I have a glass of water? I asked.

—How about a beer?

—No thanks. It's too early. Water will be just fine.

He returned with a glass, and I could see how he studied me as I drank. I turned and smiled at him.

—That hit the spot, I said.

I looked for something that wasn't too heavy, and caught sight of a brown wooden box beside the stereo. There were black, hieroglyph-like letters on the lid.

—That's Igor, Jakob said.

I could see a few yellowed bones and the crown of a skull. I pushed the lid in place and carried the box out with my arms stretched, carefully, so that it wouldn't rattle.

When we got to the wardrobe, Jakob glanced at his watch.

—Twenty minutes, he said.

I grabbed the bottom, and as we wedged it through the door, our eyes met. It occurred to me that it'd been a long time since I'd seen his eyes lit up this way. It must be the shock, I thought. Right when it happens, you don't feel a thing.

—Watch your fingers, I said as we angled the wardrobe around the corner and into the entryway.

Finally there was only the TV left, and I took that. I saw Jakob getting out a notepad and I guessed he would write a note to Helene. There were only five minutes to go, so I made sure that everything was securely fastened, and stayed by the van.

He ran out carrying his windbreaker.

I had just started the van when he remembered the keys. He worked his fingers feverishly to slide the keys from the ring. Then he got out and ran back to the apartment with them. I glanced up the street, but Helene was nowhere in sight.

We reached the first light. We sat waiting and suddenly I could sense it. I followed Jakob's glance until I saw her on the sidewalk on the opposite side of the street. It was striking how much she looked like herself; she wore a short, red jacket and tight blue pants. I saw how she pulled the hair from her face, how she shook her head very lightly, her curly blond hair bobbing up and down. Neither of us said a word. We passed within a few feet of her and she didn't see us.

This is rather unexpected, I said.

We had driven in silence for a few minutes. Jakob turned and looked at me. It was rush hour, and I kept my eyes on the traffic.

—Yeah, he said.

He sat with a foot propped up on the dashboard.

—Is it...your decision, or...is it hers?

—It's mostly mine, he said.

I looked at him, curious.

We drove on for a while without speaking. Then I looked at him again. His eyes were squinted into slits because of the sun.

—How'd she take it?

—Watch out!

A bus squeezed in ahead of us, and I hit the brake—harder than it was actually necessary. I could hear something shifting in the back, but nothing crashed down. We both turned to look, but with the piles of boxes blocking the little cab window, we couldn't see anything. Jakob said:

—I think it's all right. Let's just keep going.

We continued, and soon after I said:

—How'd she take it?

Jakob turned his head and looked at me. Then he looked out the front window again.

—All right.

I veered into the left lane, then shifted gear and turned the corner.

—It all sounds a little rash, I said.

—We've got to turn left up here.

We turned from the heavily congested road and onto a quiet street with a speed bump and three-story houses on either side. There was a Laundromat, an old-fashioned greengrocer, and a second-hand store.

Jakob pointed at a white building on the corner.

—It's over here.

I pulled the emergency brake and remained in the van. Jakob had already opened the door.

—It looks like a nice neighborhood, I said.

When we had carried everything upstairs, we each sat on a box in the middle of the apartment's largest room.

—I don't know, I said. Have I ever told you why I got divorced from my first wife?

—I don't think so, Jakob said.

I took a swig from my beer.

—It's an odd story, actually.

Jakob tipped his bottle to his mouth and closed his eyes as he drank.

—I happened to read her diary.

I set my eyes directly on Jakob.

—Most of what was in it was relatively banal. I remember that I thought: have I really married a woman who writes so badly? The way she formulated her ideas was so clumsy, I thought, almost childlike. Here and there she had made little drawings, a grumpy face, a happy face. But I kept reading.

Jakob looked down at his shoes.

—And that's how I discovered that she'd had an affair. As far as I could tell, it was over, but I was furious and beside myself and didn't know what to do. At the same time, I was pretty embarrassed that I'd found her out in that way.

I paused, and Jakob rose and walked to the window.

—I just got my things together and moved out.

Jakob stood a moment looking out; then he turned around. He blushed slightly. He had a vertical crease between his brows, which I recognized from myself.

I could feel the warmth rising to my cheeks and lowered my eyes to a spot in the middle of his chest.

I stood and went to him. I put my arm around his back and squeezed him. I could see all the way to the street where the van was parked.

—Listen, Jakob said, and worked himself free. I'm the one who's the asshole here. It's me who's found someone else.

I looked at him.

—Oh.

I stood there for a moment, staring at the roof of the van. Then I pulled myself away and went back to the box and sat down.

—Tell me, I said.

—There's not much to tell. She's sweet. Dorthe is her name. But it's pretty new. I've only known her for three weeks. There's not much to tell.

—Okay.

I finished my beer, and a moment later I stood to leave.

—Oh my, I said.

—It's all right, Jakob said and smiled.

walked to the van. It was parked underneath a tall chestnut tree, and a green chestnut lay on the roof. I stood on my tippy-toes and clutched it carefully. I turned and glanced up at the apartment. Jakob stood in the window talking on the telephone; he raised his right arm and ran his hand through his hair. I raised mine and waved.

t was just getting dark when I got home. I parked the van in front of the neighbor's house and tossed the key in his mailbox as we'd arranged. I went up the walk to my own house and saw the light in the living room. The TV was turned on.

I let myself in the utility room and cast a glance at the day's mail, which lay on the table just inside the door.

I went into the living room to my wife and put the green chestnut on the table in front of her. She raised her head and looked at me questioningly.

—Jakob said to say hello.

I went upstairs into the bedroom and stood in the middle of the room staring into space for a while. Then I went downstairs again.

—How'd it go? she asked.

—All right, I said.

I sat down beside her on the sofa. She glanced back and forth from me to the TV. Then she kept her eyes focused on the TV. The chestnut lay on the table where I'd left it. I reached for it. I pressed my thumbs into the narrow crevice and opened the shell, then set the green hemispheres on the table. The chestnut felt so unexpectedly soft and smooth in my fingers; it reminded me of something I'd once felt when I looked at my wife. I turned to her. Her stare was fixed on the television screen, the reflected image compressed and unclear on each lens of her glasses.

I continued to look at her, but it didn't help. At some point she must've noticed my desperation, because she said:

—What is it, Thomas?

Then I turned and looked towards the screen.

Crossing

You know who gave the shortest speech ever recorded?

Sophus sat on a bench in the sun. The man who'd asked this question was about seventy years old, well dressed, and had sat down beside him only a few minutes earlier. He had carefully groomed white hair, a suntan, and a soft, bulbous nose that angled slightly up.

—No, Sophus said. I don't know.

—It was Mao. He stood before the entire Chinese army on one bank of the Yangtze River, with the Japanese on the other side. When you cross this river now, Mao said, you will make history. Time will prove whether you are worthy. Then he bowed deeply to his soldiers and gave his general orders to start the battle. Isn't that something?

Sophus nodded.

—Sure, he said.

—You know what, the man continued. Sometimes I like to imagine that it's me standing in front of all those soldiers. Thousands, hundreds of thousands of soldiers and every one of them facing me. Do you know what I mean?

—I guess, Sophus said.

—Once in a while, I like to imagine I'm Hitler. I've read everything there is to read about World War II, and sometimes I pretend that I handle the whole thing differently. I avoid all the mistakes Hitler made.

Sophus stared at the briefcase the man had placed under the bench. Maybe he's got a pistol in that briefcase, he thought.

—Kjaerulf, the man said, extending his hand. Peter Kjaerulf.

Then Sophus got up and left.

That same evening, after they'd eaten dinner, Sophus asked Claudia if she'd ever fantasized about being another person.

—During puberty, she said. I wanted to be a boy.

—What about now?

—I don't know. Why?

—I met this guy in the park. He talked about being Chairman Mao and Hitler. It got me thinking.

—He sounds like a loony.

—Yeah, he was. At least in a way. But what about you? Don't you ever imagine something along those lines?

—Um.

Claudia left the room to get her cigarettes. She had a sly grin on her face when she returned.

Sophus poured them each more wine.

—Sometimes I pretend I'm being interviewed on TV.

They laughed.

—How?

—Usually it's when I'm standing in front of the mirror getting dressed. It varies, the type of program. Often it's something like *This is Your Life*. The host asks me how I like my job or my parents, or you. Could be anything.

—And how do you answer?

—It varies.

—How?

—It depends on the question. And how I feel that day.

Claudia smiled, but there was an almost imperceptible flicker of hesitation in her eyes.

—But you're still you. You don't pretend you're someone else?

—No, I don't think so. Not as far as I can recall. Well, wait a sec. Sometimes I do imagine, actually, that I'm a famous actress or television star, something like that. They show clips from all the things I've been in. I talk about my marriages, my children. Whether it's *me*, I can't really say. But what about you? Do you ever pretend such things?

—No. Sophus shook his head.

—You're sure?

—Yeah.

—Not even when you were a teenager?

He shook his head.

—Maybe you've just forgotten.

—I don't think so.

Sophus poured more wine, and Claudia went to the bathroom. In a moment she returned and sat down.

They drank in silence.

Then she said:

—I thought of something.

—Yes?

—I don't think I've ever told anyone.

—Go on, Sophus said. He'd run out of cigarettes, so he cadged one of Claudia's.

—This is back when I lived with Jens. You know, he wasn't very big and we fit into each other's clothes. He had a really expensive suit that he wore in court.

She pulled another cigarette from her pack. It was bent, and she straightened it out between two thin fingers.

—Every now and then, on some afternoon when I was bored, or if I missed him, I put the suit on. Sometimes I also put on his shirt, socks, and shoes. Even his aftershave. Then I walked around the apartment smoking cigarettes. Maybe opened a bottle of wine, too. It was like falling in love all over again. It gave me that same tingling and restless feeling. It was really odd.

Claudia sat with her cigarette still in her hand.

—And then what? Sophus asked.

—I would fantasize that I would keep the suit on until he came home, and then push him into the bedroom and tear off his clothes. You know, swap roles. I even went so far as to imagine putting a dress on him, and sexy underwear. But it was mostly a joke, of course.

—Did you ever do it?

—Once. But it wasn't very successful. It didn't turn him on. It's probably natural. Sometimes fantasies should stay fantasies.

Claudia lit her cigarette, and they sat for a while in silence, smoking. Smoke curled around their heads.

—This is your life, Sophus said. Good story.

—It's pretty far out there, isn't it?

—I'll say!

A few days later, Sophus went to get a haircut. The barber ran his hand through Sophus's shoulder-length hair and asked what Sophus wanted done.

—I don't really know.

—A page boy?

Sophus looked at himself in the mirror.

—I could also just trim it.

Sophus stared at himself.

—You know what, he said. Cut it all off.

—Super short?

—No, shaved.

The barber tousled his hair.

—Are you sure?

Sophus nodded.

The barber shifted his weight from one leg to the other and looked at Sophus in the mirror. Then he went and got the little black trimmer with steel teeth.

In one long, calm stroke he removed a strip of hair across Sophus' head. Then he moved slightly to the left and repeated the same motion.

Sophus looked in the mirror and watched his hair fall to the floor in long, feather-like tufts. Soon one half of his head was white and shaved.

The barber shifted position and Sophus felt a light pressure against his shoulder. He closed his eyes and imagined that it was Claudia cutting his hair. He imagined that it was the pressure from her vulva that he felt.

When the barber turned off the clipper, Sophus opened his eyes to his white crown.

—Now I hope you don't regret this, the barber said.

Kramer

In the building on the other side of the square there's an apartment where the light is always on. A bare bulb hangs in one of the rooms, and it has been on for as long as Kaspar and I have lived here. When I wake at night, or if we come home late, I glance over there to see if it is still turned on.

Why don't they turn off the light? I always wonder.

The apartment is too far away for me to see who lives there; sometimes I'm not even sure anyone lives there at all. Yet I often find myself looking over there.

One afternoon as I stood by the window, I heard a strange noise in the hallway. I stepped over the creaky board in the entryway and leaned carefully against the door. With my fingers I pushed the little cap away from the peephole. At first I couldn't see anything—it was nearly dark in the hallway—but then I noticed a crumpled figure sitting halfway down the stairwell. It was our upstairs neighbor, Mr. Kramer. He sat hunched over, with his arms crossed at the knee and his white head resting on his arms. The sound I'd heard was a low, irregular snore.

I opened the door and stepped into the hallway, and stood looking at him. I don't know how much time passed, five minutes, maybe more. Suddenly he stopped snoring and lifted his head and looked at me.

—Oh, he said. Is it you?

—Mr. Kramer, I said. Don't you think you should go to bed?

—Yes, he said.

Then his head fell forward again. Some time passed. This time he didn't snore.

—Mr. Kramer, I said.

—Yes? he said, sleepily, surprised.

—You shouldn't sleep here.

—No.

Then he rose and I could tell he wasn't really awake. He stood swaying in the middle of the stairwell.

—Grab the banister, I said.

I turned on the light and kept my finger on the switch so it wouldn't click off again. I could see a wet stain on the stairs where he'd been sitting. I could also see a big, dark spot on the seat of his pants. He squeezed the banister with both hands and started up the stairs, one step at a time.

—You okay? I said.

—Oh yes, he said. I'm okay.

I went back into my apartment and filled a bucket with soap and water.

When I returned to the stairwell, he was sitting on the top step. He sat with his head between his long legs, and he looked as though he might fall over at any moment. I set the bucket down and climbed up to him; I jostled his arm lightly.

—Yeah? he said.

—Come on.

I extended my hand and helped him get up. He put his arm around my neck, with his other arm on the banister, supporting himself.

When we'd climbed a few steps, he stopped and looked at me.

—It's awfully nice of you to do this, he said.

—It's all right, I said.

—I mean it, he said. It's really nice of you.

We continued our climb. He felt heavier with each step.

—We're almost there, I said.

He stopped again.

—Can I ask you something?

—Sure, I said.

—How old are you?

—I'm twenty five.

—Oh, he said. So young.

After we'd reached the landing, he stopped and searched his pockets. He still had his arm around me.

—Can I offer you anything?

—No thanks.

—I mean it, he said.

—You need to get some sleep.

—No, he said. I can always do that.

I pulled away from his arm.

—Another time, I said, smiling.

I went back down.

I picked up the bucket at the foot of the stairs and began cleaning up. I dried the puddle halfway up the stairs, and as I was about to clean the mess from his wet pants at the top of the stairwell, I realized that he was still standing in front of his door.

—Mr. Kramer, I said. Go to bed now.

—Oh, he said.

—Mr. Kramer, I said.

That's when I saw his hand working the crotch of his pants. At that same moment he turned, and I met his triumphant stare as he ejaculated onto the stairs. He held my gaze. His eyes suddenly seemed yellow; it was a little like seeing into a cat's eyes.

Then I rushed down the stairs.

For a long time I stood by the window in the kitchen looking toward the apartment on the other side of the square. Above me, I could hear his feet dragging across the floor. Then I heard the sound of glass or porcelain shattering, followed by a thump, and then complete silence.

I stood listening for some time. I could hear a toilet flush somewhere in the building, and through the closed window I could hear the cooing of the doves on the roof.

Maybe he's dead, I thought, and wondered whether I should go up and check on him, but I didn't.

When Kaspar got home, I told him what had happened.

—What a pig, he said and went upstairs. I could hear his knuckles rapping against Kramer's door. Soon after, he came back down.

—He won't open the door, he said.

—Maybe we should do something? I said a little later, when we'd sat down to dinner.

—We could turn him in.

—It sounded as if he fell. Maybe he's hurt.

—He probably just dropped something.

After dinner when Kaspar turned on the TV, I went into the kitchen. I stood by the window looking over toward the apartment on the other side of the square. The sharp light tinted the trees blue and left a vague reflection on the wet square. I remained standing, watching. I let the light and the emptiness from the apartment seep into me, until I felt completely empty and free. I don't know how long I stood there, but suddenly I saw something move, a shadow, an outline of a person. Nothing more than that, but it was enough that I stepped from the window and out of sight.

The next morning, after Kaspar had gone to work, I went upstairs and knocked on the door. No one answered and I opened the mail slot to have a look inside; I could see the entrance and a corner of the kitchen.

—Mr. Kramer, I said.

Then I caught sight of him; he lay on the kitchen floor. I could see his brown shoes and a small band of his socks. I could see shards of green glass on the floor. Carefully I closed the mail slot and went back downstairs.

When I heard the ambulance, I braced myself against my door and put my eye to the little round peephole. I saw a policeman, and then two paramedics and a man in overalls, who I guessed was the locksmith. The two paramedics carried a stretcher.

In a little while they came back down with Mr. Kramer. A blanket covered his body and they took their time.

—Well, the locksmith said, you guys have probably seen it all.

—Oh yes, one of the paramedics said.

The second paramedic added something that I couldn't hear, but I heard the men laugh.

The policeman came down the stairs and stopped in front of my door. I watched his hand rise toward the door, and I heard him knock, I stood completely still and pressed my body against the door. My heart thumped so loudly that for one moment I was afraid the policeman would hear it.

He knocked two more times, waited a moment, and then he left.

That same evening I told the story to Kaspar. He sat on the sofa, and I was standing.

He said:

—You know, he probably would have died no matter what.

—You don't know that, I said.

—He was eighty years old.

—So?

—He was a pig.

I turned and went out to the kitchen. I stood beside the window and looked across to the apartment on the other side of the square.

Later, as we lay in bed, Kaspar said:

—Every second somebody dies somewhere. Now it just happened to be someone upstairs.

—So you're saying that I didn't do anything wrong?

—Absolutely nothing wrong.

—You're sure?

—Yes, he said. Of course I'm sure.

—I hope you're right, I said.

I huddled close to him, and that's how we lay for a while. He got on top of me, and I let him spread my legs.

When he came, I saw Kramer. I saw his sperm arcing out over the stairs, and I saw his eyes.

—Is something wrong? Kaspar asked afterwards.

I shook my head.

He wouldn't understand, I thought.

Hair

Mette is standing on the scale brushing her teeth. Frands is watching the needle tremble in rhythm with her movements. She steps off the scale, her back to him, and goes to the sink. He sees her expressionless face in the mirror. In her left hand she gathers up her hair, bends forward, and spits a jet of pink foam into the sink. Then she puts down the toothbrush and looks up. Frands' first impulse is to avoid catching her glance in the mirror, but he forces himself not to.

—Mette, he says.

She walks past him and into the hall.

For a moment, he's left with his own reflection. Then he follows her into the bedroom. She's already in bed, her face to the wall. He stands at the window looking out. A car is parked under a streetlight and he can see two people sitting inside. He can't tell whether it's anyone they know.

—Mette?

—Stop saying my name.

—Listen to me, he says.

—I *have* forgiven you. Let's not talk about it anymore.

—Okay, he says.

Frands sees the neighbor's daughter exit the car and walk toward the house. Before she opens the front door, she turns and waves. The car starts and slowly begins to roll away. Lights snap on in the house, and he follows her journey from room to room. Finally, the only light on in the house is on the top floor, to the right.

—Then sleep well.

—Where are you going? she asks.

—I'm just going to have a drink. Then I'll be up.

Frands goes downstairs and sits on the couch. The bottle of cognac is on the coffee table. He warms the glass in his hand for a while before he drinks. The liquid feels soft in his mouth. There's a slimy gray clump in the center of the table, residue from the washing machine's filter. He pulls a long black hair from the clump and lays it beside the others Mette has already pulled out. He drains his glass and refills it. It's warm in the living room.

He takes his glass and the bottle and goes out to his studio. He sits on a stool. Through the skylight he can trace the outline of the pear trees' upper branches, which reach over the house. There's no moon, yet a small glow of light is still thrown though the large window frames. He can see his granite towering in the center of his studio, unfinished, more stone than sculpture. And he can see all of the small figures—Mette calls them children— many of them just as unfinished.

Frands stands and goes out to the yard. Yellow apples lie in the grass. He walks into the garage looking for something to sit on and finds an old recliner. With some effort he hauls it outside. He sits facing the house and takes a nip from the bottle. He lets his eyes wander over the house's whitewashed façade. Even in the half-dark it seems stained and porous, and he can see spots where the plaster has been cracked by frost. The real estate agent had talked for a long time about how charming the house was. An artist villa, he'd called it. With space for children. It was exactly what they were looking for, Mette had said.

Frands lets his eyes wander up toward the bedroom, sees the curtains have yet to be drawn closed. Just then there's a noise in the shrubbery behind the garage. He glares into the tangled darkness. A short while later the neighbor's cat pops out from the bush further up, near the house. He tries to lure the cat to him by hissing at it, but it crosses the yard and disappears in the tall grass on the other side.

When he glances up again, he sees Mette in the window. She stands completely motionless, her arms resting at her side, gazing out as if she's in a trance. Frands gets the feeling she's staring at a point far in the distance. He considers getting up or waving, but the longer he waits, the more awkward it feels. Ten minutes pass, maybe more, then she steps back and draws the curtains closed. Relieved, he sinks back into the chair. He can hear the train rattle toward the city. He lifts the bottle and leans his head back.

Frands has almost emptied the bottle when his eyes slide shut. Immediately, the image of his neighbor's house appears in his mind. He sees the windows light up one after the other and hears the daughter humming while she walks through the house. Her humming rises in intensity as she walks, grows more disharmonious, uneven; halfway up the stairs she breaks into song. By the time she snaps on the light in the last room, she's screaming.

The sky is getting light when Frands opens his eyes. With difficulty he rises from the chair. He can feel the cold in his bones and makes his way, stiff-legged, toward the house. He grabs the doorknob and realizes it's locked. He takes a few steps backward and looks up toward the dormer. The curtains are still closed. Then he remembers which way he came. He walks around to the side of the house where the door of his studio is ajar.

Mette doesn't react when he crawls under the duvet. He has kept his clothes on and stares up at the ceiling; the light in the room is pale and gray. Slowly he warms up.

—Is it someone I know? Mette asks suddenly.

Frands hesitates a moment.

—No, he says.

—What's her name?

—Kate, he says.
—Is she beautiful?
Frands hesitates again.
—Yes, he says. She's beautiful.

Unsettled

Tobias had sent five poems to his old teacher. They were very short and had been published in a literary journal. One of them was about the moon: a man had been unfaithful to his wife and he cursed at the moon because he felt guilty every time he looked at it.

A few weeks later his old teacher called him. He had moved, he explained, and invited Tobias to come visit him.

When the day arrived, Tobias borrowed his sister's car and drove away from the city. It was in the afternoon. The sun was low on the horizon, and the cars cast long shadows. On the highway he drove west, and after twenty-five miles he changed direction heading north and continued on increasingly smaller roads. He had studied the map carefully and found his destination without great difficulty: it was a little white house that lay at the foot of a hill.

He parked the car to the right of the house, and Erik came out and greeted him. They shook hands and remained standing a moment looking out over the fields. Erik was tall and thin; Tobias only reached his shoulders.

—It's beautiful here, Tobias said. His teacher turned his head and smiled at him. He was tanned. His eyes were narrow; his blue irises hung in a net of small veins.

—Come on in, he said.

In the kitchen the table was set, and they sat down. Erik poured tea and offered Tobias a piece of honey cake from an oval plate. Tobias caught a glimpse of his poems on the counter in front of the breadbox.

Erik asked what he was up to, and Tobias explained that he'd dropped out of the university; that he was at work on a collection of poems. Erik told him he'd retired five years earlier.

—I was lucky, he said.

He'd retired because of back problems, but a year later he'd had an operation.

—I got a chance to start a new life.

He went on telling Tobias how he'd found the house, and how the deal was made; Tobias drank his tea and glanced now and then at the breadbox.

After some time, Erik rose and placed his cup in the sink.

—Let me show you around, he said.

The house was sparsely furnished. In the living room there was a loveseat and a coffee table. The second floor was divided into two rooms of equal size. In the first a bed stood along one wall; in the other a telescope was set up under a skylight.

Tobias put an eye to the telescope and looked up into the blue spring sky.

—There's too much light, Erik said.

They put on their jackets and went out to the driveway.

—I'm planting flowers.

Erik made his way to the southern end of the house. There was a cardboard box with white and blue petunias inside, five of them already planted.

—Pretty, aren't they?

—Sure, Tobias said. Absolutely.

On the eastern side of the house was a little garden with a few fruit trees, and bordering the garden was a low stone wall. The grass was yellow, in some patches almost white. They went through an opening in the stone wall and walked along a path that ran near the foot of the hill. Tobias asked Erik what had happened to his book collection.

—I've sold it, Erik said, calmly.

He explained how he'd tried to donate it to several libraries, but none of them had any room for it. He'd made an offer to the county that they could buy his house and move the library there, but they'd politely declined. So he'd sold the collection to an antiquarian, and it had taken two men a whole week to empty the house.

They came to a green building behind the hill; it resembled a garage or a barn. The path edged closely past it, and Erik stopped and shoved the door open. He turned on the light. The room was about twenty by twenty feet, and, in the middle of the recently swept floor, underneath fluorescent bulbs, there was a ping pong table.

Tobias looked at his teacher.

On either end of the table lay a paddle; under one of the paddles was a ball.

—Do you want to play? Erik asked.

Tobias went over to the table. He took up the paddle and felt its weight in his hand. Erik had taken position on the opposite side of the table. He stood ready with the paddle and ball.

—Okay, Tobias said.

Erik played. His serve was short and low, and Tobias sent it directly into the net.

—1-0, Erik said.

He served again. This time Tobias struck the ball over the net, but it came back immediately.

—2-0, Erik said.

The third time Tobias managed to hit the ball a few times, but then Erik smashed the ball past him.

—3-0.

On the fourth and fifth serves Erik aced him, and then it was Tobias's turn. Erik stood in the same place and returned his serves.

—0-6.

—0-7.

—0-8.

—0-9.

—0-10.

—10-0, Erik said. Before long he'd won the match. Then they changed sides, and the same performance was repeated. Once or twice Tobias tried to start a conversation.

When they were out in the daylight again, Tobias was dripping with sweat. Erik closed the door, and Tobias looked at him.

—It was here when I moved in, he said.

The hill was behind them now, and they continued past the fields. Erik pointed at a utility pole where he had seen an owl. He pointed at a large farm a good distance away.

—That's my closest neighbor, he said.

They passed a cluster of tall trees, and then they came to a small lake. On the bank was a boat landing, but no boat.

They stood in silence and stared across the water.

—Lay down, Erik said.

Surprised, Tobias looked at him.

—You've got to see between the second and third boards.

Tobias glanced from the boat landing to Erik.

—Go ahead, Erik said.

Reluctantly, Tobias lay down on the cold landing. The green boards were slightly damp. He positioned himself so he could see between the second and third boards.

It was like looking through a piece of clear glass. The bottom was covered in rotten leaves. There were tangles of vegetation, and Tobias could see a long translucent string with small black eggs inside. He could see a yellow-brown mussel. Where it had inched along, it had left behind a thin, white trail in the sand. He raised his head and looked at Erik. Erik stood on the shore of the lake staring beneath the dock; he didn't look up, and Tobias sensed that Erik wanted him to be patient. So he stared at the water again.

He looked at the mussel. It had not moved. He traced its trail across the sandy bottom and then looked at the black fish eggs. A school of tiny fish flickered through his field of vision. They hovered right below him; they were almost transparent and their fins were tinged with red.

At that moment a huge fish glided beneath the dock. Tobias couldn't see the whole thing at once: only its gills and part of its back. Its skin was light green and dotted with yellow spots. It moved a bit, and a large round eye the size of a quarter came into view.

Tobias pulled back instinctively. He turned to get Erik's attention, but Erik wasn't there. Tobias got on his knees and scanned the lake. Then he bent forward slowly and looked at the water again.

The fish was still. Tobias stared at the black iris and the yellow-green circle around it. The eye didn't blink. He could make out a number of small, spiked teeth in the front of its mouth.

He rose. He moved onto the path searching for his teacher.

—Erik, he called.

No answer. Tobias walked along the sodden path.

He went to the other side of the lake and stood a moment looking toward the boat landing.

He called out again.

When he returned to the boat landing, the sky had begun to darken. He made his way back the same way they had come. He saw light in the neighbor's house; he shivered a little when he passed the darkened barn.

There were no lights on in Erik's house. Moving swiftly, Tobias went up to the front door. He grabbed at the doorknob and discovered that it was locked. He tried again; then he turned and walked to the car. He leaned against the driver's side door.

He couldn't have fallen in the lake, he thought.

He remained standing. In a little while the moon rose behind the hill. It was almost full and seemed unnaturally large. The light was so strong that he could see the box of flowers at the end of the house. He could see the stone wall and the path that led to the barn. The moon spilled light into the car, and Tobias spotted something white on the front seat. He opened the door and gathered up the five pages. They hadn't been touched. There were no corrections, no commentary. They hardly even appeared to have been read.

He climbed into the car and sat down.

He watched the house. Through the window on the second floor he could make out the telescope. He couldn't see Erik, but he knew he was there.

Then he started the car.

Intercom

Jess wakes up because Maria is talking in her sleep.

—Yeah, she says, followed by a stream of words he doesn't catch. He watches her turn on her side and then on her stomach. Now she clutches the pillow, her black hair matted and spread across the white pillow cover. Jess observes her in the dark. He can just make out her lips, which sleep has made big and soft. She swallows, and makes a barely audible lip-smack.

—Oh, Markus, she mumbles.

Jess drops his head on the pillow. Soon he throws off the duvet and sets his feet on the cold floor. He goes into the living room and sits in the green chair. Then he stands and goes into the kitchen. Maria's purse rests on the table. He unclasps it and carefully removes its contents. He opens her date book, skims a few months back, and finally examines her list of telephone numbers. He studies a little compact with mirror and powder. He unfolds wrinkled-up papers and presses them flat, telephone messages, receipts, and a napkin with an impression of her lips. Then he puts it all back in the purse and goes into the living room and sits in the green chair.

Jess remains seated for an hour. When he's ice cold he crawls back into bed.

Next morning he gets up before Maria and goes to work.

Jess spends the morning at his office. He moves the stack of papers around and starts over on the same letter three times. At 9:30 he sees an older woman waving a yellow cloth from a window in the building across the street. A little while later, in the neighboring apartment, the curtains part to reveal a young woman talking on the telephone; when she opens the window and leans out, the light dazzles Jess for a moment. Still talking, the woman glances down at the street. In the apartment on her left, the older woman vacuums. At 1 p.m. Jess calls the switchboard and tells them he's sick.

When he steps out on the street, he notices that it's still cold, even though it's the middle of the day. It's early spring; the light is sharp but brings with it no warmth. Two glaziers balance a shop window, and Jess stops to watch. He stands there until he's emptied of feeling, completely overwhelmed by the light, and then he goes on.

Jess walks into a café and finds a table by the window; the waiter walks past with a clinking tray filled with glasses, and Jess orders a beer. Two girls sit at his right; one has short, dark hair and gentle eyes; the other is blond, with sharp eyes. The blond girl has a little silver heart around her throat and leans over, confiding in her friend in a hushed voice. Jess opens the newspaper that's on the table. The waiter serves his beer with a prissy smile, and Jess reads and drinks. Then he stares out at the square. He gazes at the bare benches and at a few transparent plastic bags lazily swept up in the wind; he watches as they're emptied and filled with air and shot through with sunlight.

Jess finds a shiny twenty-kroner coin in his wallet and puts it on the table. When he opens the door, he turns and casts a final glance at the two girls. The dark-haired one sits listening patiently, the back of her hand under her chin, while the blond leans so far across the table the little silver heart almost touches the surface.

Not long after that, Jess is standing in front of his apartment building. The intercom is broken; he can hear it scratching and crackling in the speaker. He puts his key in the door, but pulls it out again. He puts his finger on the white button instead.

—Yes? Maria answers a moment later.

Jess presses his scarf to his mouth.

—It's Markus.

—Who is it?

Jess leans closer to the microphone.

—Markus.

The lock buzzes, and he pushes the door open with his foot. On his way up he meets his downstairs neighbor.

—Hello, Jess, he says as he passes.

—Hello, Anders, Jess says and squeezes his keys hard.

When he finally reaches the third floor, the door to his apartment is ajar. Jess pushes it open and sees Maria in the kitchen; she turns and smiles.

—Hey, baby.

Jess notices that she's wearing a new shirt.

It's a little small, and he can see a strip of her belly. She comes to him, plants a quick kiss on his lips.

—There's something wrong with the intercom. I couldn't hear anything.

Jess studies Maria for a long moment. Then he hangs his scarf and his jacket in the entryway, walks into the living room, and sits at the long table. Maria follows him.

—Have you had a good day?

—Yes, thanks.

—Would you like coffee?

—Sure, why not?

Maria goes into the kitchen and puts on the water and returns quickly. She sets two cups on the table along with a little glass pitcher of milk. Then she gets behind him and runs her fingers through his short, bristly hair.

—I didn't hear you leave this morning. How did you manage not to wake me?

He raises his shoulders and lets them fall.

—You were sleeping soundly.

—I was in fact. It felt great to sleep in.

Maria's hands continue down to his chest and pry a button on his shirt, and one hand slips underneath. Jess can feel her belly against the back of his head. Then she bends forward and he can feel her breasts. She nips softly at his ear.

—Maybe we should hold off on the coffee for a little while? she says.

—Maybe we should, he says.

Rose

W e lay in our beds counting the miles. Lightning flashed and I could see Morten against the far wall. I saw his lips moving and could tell he was counting to himself. Before anything happened, lightning flashed twice. Then came thunder, a whole series, gradually drawing closer, and then an abundance of lightning and the rain drummed against the roof. Morten's voice sounded weak:

—There are too many. I can't tell which thunder goes with which lightning.

I could hear in his voice that he was about to cry, and I thought he might start asking a lot of questions. Like where Mom was, almost a week had gone by now, and why didn't Dad come home, and Grandpa—who was supposed to look after us while Grandma was out searching—where was he?

—Can I lie next to you? he asked.

Through another bolt of lightning I saw his pale face and took pity on him.

—Okay, I said.

Then he crawled out of his bed and into mine. He lay close to me, motionless and quiet.

Not long after, he fell asleep.

W e didn't see Grandpa until late morning the next day. We were sitting at the kitchen table eating toasted cheese sandwiches when a blue Rover pulled into the driveway. It was the second Rover this week. Two nights earlier he'd driven a red one. A moment later he stood in the door.

—Why aren't you two in school?

His cream-colored suit was wrinkled, and what was left of his hair formed a wooly halo atop his head.

—We don't have any milk money, I said.

—Where have you been? Morten asked him.

Grandpa pawed through his jacket and found two ten kroner coins, which he handed to us.

—Now get going, he said.

I could tell that Morten was about to ask again, so I elbowed him.

—Come on, I said.

The teacher smiled wearily and a little sadly at us as we snuck into the classroom and slid into our seats in the back. As soon as we sat down I saw Rose turn her fresh pink cheeks and look at Morten, who stared at his desk, embarrassed.

For some reason, we were spared that day. Every now and then the teacher glanced at us, but passed us over and made others read aloud and calculate math problems on the chalkboard. As usual, Morten wrote letters to Rose. He never dared give them to her; he was never quite satisfied and crumpled them up one after the other as he wrote new letters, which would also end up in his bag. *Sweet flower, my Rose, prettier than anyone.* That's how all the letters began. I sat staring at her long hair and felt warm all over.

We got to go home early, but we stayed to see if anything fun would happen. Tommy told a story about his cousin, who'd gotten a pair of pointy-toed cowboy boots with iron tips. He had worn them on the first day of school, and had booted one of the small kids right in the ass so hard that the little muscle that sits up there popped and the boy's intestines had fallen out.

Instead of riding home, we went into town. At the grocery store we each bought a water pistol with Grandpa's money.

Afterwards we rode past Rose's. A whole row of girls' bikes was lined up outside, but there was no one in the yard or behind the windows in the big house. For a while we stood leaning against the picket fence. Suddenly the curtain was thrust back, and fat Lilly's face appeared. I gave her the finger, and she disappeared, but immediately the curtain was pushed back and a line of new faces appeared. Rose wasn't there, I made faces at them and waited for her to show up. I peered down the street, first toward the train tracks and then toward the grocery store. When the coast was clear, I yanked down my pants. I pulled out my dick and stuck it in between the white slats. The curtain wavered, and more faces appeared, all watching me pee with my arms folded over the fence, my dick jammed between the slats. When I was done, I pulled my pants back up and drifted over to my bike.

Morten had already ridden off. He kept a few hundred feet ahead all the way home and wouldn't stop, even when I yelled at him.

When I got home, his bike lay in the driveway.

Grandpa sat in the kitchen eating a toasted cheese sandwich and drinking one of Dad's beers. He wore the same cream suit and didn't look any better than he had in the morning. Five or six empty bottles were arranged next to one of the table legs, and beside another, five or six unopened bottles.

—There are more in the freezer.

He took a bite with his all too white teeth and nodded at the fridge; the door was ajar. I wasn't hungry so I went upstairs to see if Morten was up there reading his comic books; that's what he normally did after school. It was none of my business, but for whatever reason I couldn't let him be. Maybe it was because of Rose, maybe it was because he was my brother, or maybe it was because of what happened—or what *didn't* happen. All we were doing was waiting. Morten wasn't in his room, so I went downstairs again.

The blue Rover was in the driveway. All the doors were locked, but the right front window was not rolled all the way up.

I put my hand then my whole arm inside and down to the door lock. The radio was one of those kinds that could be turned on without the key, so I sat for a while listening to the radio and forgot all about Morten. It was late in the summer, and there were stubbly fields in every direction. In other years Dad had allowed us to drive down to the bog and back. The first years he'd helped us with the gears, but after a while we did it ourselves.

I snuck from the car and went into the kitchen. Grandpa sat still on his chair draining beers, which he picked up from one table leg and set down at the other. The keys lay on the table between us.

—Where's Morten? he asked. Didn't you come home from school together?

—He's sitting in the car, I said.

Grandpa stood, a little shakily, but he stood.

When he'd gone out the door, I grabbed the keys and followed slowly behind. We met halfway.

—I don't want you two messing with my car, he said.

Then he disappeared inside the house again.

Morten fanned his arms wildly as I drove across the yard. I stopped the car and picked him up.

—Did he let you drive it?

—Yeah, I said.

We continued down through the yard and into the field. We had just come out onto the stubble when I caught sight of the neighbor's dog. It was sniffing around on our side of the property line. It had once bitten Morten, so I turned sharply to the right and started after it. At first it stood staring at us dumbly, but then it took off running along the dirt road on the other side of the property line. Morten said something or other as I continued into the neighbor's field, but I ignored it. The dog was right in front of us, with its tongue wagging from its chops, bolting away, sometimes to the right, sometimes to the left of us. I jerked the steering wheel from side to side; it was not something you did unless you had such a dog in front of you. We had reached a good way across the field, so far that nobody could've seen us from home. That's when I looked at Morten. He opened his eyes wide and covered his face in his hands. I looked ahead and saw the creek. I heard Morten shout something I couldn't make out, and I could tell from the steering how the front wheels had lost contact with the ground. Suddenly we hung suspended in air, floating, but only for a moment. Then we landed on the other side of the creek. I caught the wheel in my gut, but Morten braced himself against the dashboard, so nothing happened to him. The front of the Rover didn't look so pretty, but the motor still ran.

The dog hadn't made the jump across the creek, and now it strutted on the other side, big and dumb and aggressive. We sat for a while catching our breath.

—What do you think Grandpa's gonna say? Morten asked.

I shrugged my shoulders and put the car in gear. We rolled through the grass until we found the road.

On the main road we turned right, driving away from town. We were going at a good speed when we reached the driveway to the disused gravel pit. I hit the brake, but the car braked funny and went off course. I got the car stopped and backed thirty feet; then we drove down into the pit.

We made a few passes down there, but we didn't see Tommy or Tommy's brother or anyone else.

—Tommy's full of shit, Morten said.

Tommy had told us how his big brother from 10ᵗʰ grade and two of his friends and three girls sometimes went out to the gravel pit. Tommy had snuck down there once and seen his brother's white ass on top of one of the girls.

—Just because they're not here now doesn't mean they weren't here, I said.

—I don't believe him, Morten said, especially that one about the cowboy boots.

We drove up to the main road and again away from town.

We had driven for about fifteen minutes when we spotted Dad's car rounding a curve and heading toward us. Morten ducked and I leaned on the brake. The car jerked to the side, but Dad was already far beyond us.

—Did you see if Mom was with him?

I shook my head.

I turned the Rover around and followed slowly behind. When we got to town, Dad's car was parked at the grocery store. Mom sat in the car, but she didn't see us. Morten shouted,

—Stop, damn it! Mom's with him.

I kept driving. Morten punched my shoulder, but I didn't stop. Then he sank back in his seat and fell silent, and that's how he sat the rest of the way home. We cruised into the driveway, and everything looked calm. I parked the car exactly where it had been parked, then we got out and stood there uncertainly, not knowing if we should go in. Morten went first. Grandpa wasn't in the kitchen. Empty bottles crowded one table leg, and on the table there was an opened newspaper and half-eaten toast. We found him sleeping on the couch in the living room. At that same instant we heard Dad's car crunching on the gravel. Maybe it was because of the Rover, but Morten wasn't eager to go outside and greet them. We stood reluctantly in the doorway as they came inside. Dad held Mom's suitcase, and Mom carried the bag of groceries. She looked tired. First she hugged Morten, then me.

—Aren't you glad to see your mother again?

—Where have you been? Morten asked.

Her eyes flickered.

—Now we'll see how well you've looked after the house while I was away. Where is your grandfather? Grandma went home. She's waiting for him.

When he saw all the bottles in the kitchen, Dad cursed. Then he went in and woke up Grandpa. As Grandpa went out and saw the Rover, he pointed at Morten and said that he'd made a mess of it. Dad told him he must've done it himself while he was drunk.

After dinner we watched television, and it was good to see that everything was as it used to be. We were allowed to stay up longer and watch a movie, but at 11:00 Dad said it was time for us to go to bed.

At first we could hear them shouting at each other. But then it grew quiet. We lay in the dark along each wall.

—Morten, I whispered.

He didn't respond.

—Are you asleep?

Then I heard him crying; it was hollow and dry, as if he was trying to hide it. For a while I just lay there, waiting.

—I'm not interested in Rose, I said. If you want her, she's yours.

He kept going. It sounded like he could neither cry nor quit. I climbed from the bed and crawled over to him. When I lay down I got his elbow in my stomach. I caught my breath, then crawled back to my own bed.

X-Ray

Carl and Sonja huddle together around the small table. The kitchen is warm, and it smells of fresh coffee and toast. Carl sips his coffee; Sonja has drunk most of hers.

—What time do you need to be there? she asks.

—11:00, he says.

She rises and picks up the coffee pot.

—More?

—No thanks.

She pours coffee for herself, and he reaches for a piece of toast.

—Are you sure you don't want me to come with you? she asks, returning to her seat.

—I'd rather go alone, he says. He coats his toast with orange marmalade.

She opens her calendar and finds the day: January 11, 1994.

—I had the same dream last night, Carl says.

She looks up.

He immediately regrets having told her about it.

—It bothers me, she says. I don't like the fact that you're going by yourself.

—It'll be all right, he says. I'm not nervous.

He lays his hand on hers. She looks at him. Her eyes seem larger.

—Are you sure? she asks.

—Yes, he says. I'm positive.

When Sonja has gone, Carl carries the newspaper upstairs. He lays his bathrobe over the armrest on the blue chair and crawls under the still half-warm duvet. He begins to read. He skims the news, glances at the TV program, and picks up the culture section. There's an article about Rembrandt that captures his attention. *Chiaroscuro.* He chews on the word a bit.

After reading the article, he rises from the bed and goes into Sonja's den. He pulls the encyclopedia volume that covers Q to Sve from the shelf, and returns to the bedroom. He reads the entry about Rembrandt. It lists a number of his masterpieces; the year in which they were painted is written in parentheses, along with their current location: Stockholm, Dresden, Haag, or Amsterdam. Carl regrets never having made the time to visit any of the museums named. As a young man he'd often gone to Rotterdam, and from there it would have only been an hour and a half by train to Amsterdam. Today it'd no doubt be even faster.

Carl looks at the painting that is reproduced in the encyclopedia. Its title is written in small letters under the black and white print: *Jacob Blessing the Sons of Joseph.* The painting shows an old, long-bearded man wearing a little headdress; he sits halfway up in bed extending his hand. Two small boys stand at the side of the bed; one is blond, the other dark. The old man gently touches the blond child's head. The children's parents stand behind them.

It occurs to him that even though the motif is sad, the scene is depicted with a tenderness reminiscent of happiness. Maybe it is because Jacob has lived so well and so long, so long that he can barely get up from the bed, so long that he has had grandchildren. Maybe also because the pillow that awaits Jacob's head looks so pristinely white. Carl's eyes rest on the pillow, then travel across the gray nuances in the painting's middle section to the mother's face and neck. From here they move toward the center, toward Joseph. His expression is gentle, sad, his eyes are looking down, possibly in the direction of the children; he stands near the bed, so close that it looks as though Jacob rests his forehead against his cheek.

Carl puts the book down and sticks his hand under his pajamas to probe his belly. He massages it carefully in large, circular strokes. Then he rises and goes to the bathroom. He undresses, puts out a towel, and gets in the shower. The water runs down his body, swirls into the drain, soapy and gray.

Then he hears the telephone ring.

Carl lets it ring. He turns up the cold water and turns down the warm water and can feel his skin tighten and tremble. He turns off the shower and steps out. He grabs his towel and dries his face carefully, then his belly. He can trace his own form in the full-length mirror on the back of the door. With his hand he clears a space for his face, but the mirror quickly steams up again.

After he has dressed, he goes downstairs and sits by the telephone. Outside, it has begun to snow. He dials his son Jesper's number; Jesper lives with Maria and her son, Jonas. The telephone rings a few times before someone answers.

—Hello, Carl says.

He can hear breathing on the other end of the line.

—Hello, he repeats.

—It's Jonas.

—Well, hi there, Jonas. It's Carl.

—Hi.

—How are you?

—I got chewing gum today.

—Aren't you lucky. What does it taste like?

—Like chewing gum.

—But you're doing okay?

—Uh huh.

—Is Jesper or your mother home?

—No.

—What's that mean? Are you home alone?

—Who is it? he hears Maria say in the background.

—Nobody, Jonas says, mouth turned from the receiver. Goodbye, he says.

—Bye, bye, Carl says.

—Jonas! Maria shouts.

There's a clicking as the receiver is hung up. Carl smiles and looks out the window. The snowflakes are large and downy and fall from the heavens in straight lines. He watches them settle into fine layers on the naked earth. He sees how the flakes are sifted through the branches of the chestnut tree, forming a complex pattern of snow and darkness on the ground beneath the tree.

Then he looks at his watch and rises from his chair.

Carl has been sitting in the waiting room for almost a half-hour before the doctor's assistant peers her head through the door.

—Carl Skov.

He stands and follows her down the hallway. Examination rooms are on both sides of the hall. At the far end a door is open on the right, and she leads him into the room.

—Have a seat. The doctor will be with you in a moment.

Carl sits on a brown plastic chair and looks around. In one end of the room there is an examination chair with stirrups made of stainless steel. A white paper slip covers the black cushion. On the table beside Carl is his insurance card and a form he'll have to sign. Next to that is a file with his medical records and a big yellow-brown envelope, which he can see has been opened.

Carl looks out the window. On the lawn in front of the medical center a group of children are playing in the snow. They look comfortable in their quilted snowsuits.

—Hello, Mr. Skov.

The doctor slides the door closed and extends his left hand to Carl; Carl clasps it clumsily with his right. The doctor sits in the chair and skims Carl's records. With thick, competent fingers he opens the envelope and pulls out a number of X-rays. He holds them up to the light and examines them one by one.

—So, Mr. Skov, he says. I think you're going to have to change your eating habits.

—Is that so?

—There's nothing wrong with you. The photographs here indicate that you are fine. If your stomach is bothering you, it is because of nerves or poor diet.

The doctor bends forward and picks up a piece of paper that is lying on a shelf to his left.

—Here's a list of some things I'd recommend you eat.

Carl takes the paper and reads. Soundlessly he forms the words on his lips: carrots, celery, apples, whole-grain bread, fish.

—Do you have a lot going on these days?

Carl looks up.

—Not really. Nothing more than usual.

The doctor leans back in his chair.

—Something else bothering you?

—Not really. I can't think of anything.

—Marital problems. Financial troubles? An illness in the family?

—No, nothing like that.

Carl thinks a moment.

—Well, he says. I keep dreaming of water.

—Of water?

—I dream of huge bodies of water. Almost every night.

—Any idea why?

—No, actually I don't.

Carl looks down, and neither of them speak for a moment. Then the doctor smiles and shrugs.

—Every once in a while we have to accept some things we don't understand.

—I guess so, Carl says.

The doctor leans forward clutching the form.

Carl reaches for one of the X-rays and holds it up to the light. His stomach and intestines are marked with a thin white line, the rest lies in darkness. He sees the children outside. Their snowsuits appear gold and crimson through the cloudy film.

—I just need you to sign here.

The doctor pushes the form and insurance card toward Carl.

Carl is still holding the X-ray up to the light.

—Are those your children? he asks.

The doctor looks at him, puzzled.

Carl puts the X-ray down. After he has signed, he picks it up again.

—May I keep this?

—Sure, the doctor says, looking up. But believe me, there's nothing to see.

Phosphorescence

They sat on the keel of a dinghy that was lying on the beach. Thomas was leaning back, supporting himself with his hands, head tilted, gazing up. Jon looked straight off into the night. He could see the foam of the low surf, could hear the pebbles murmuring as the water moved back out to sea.

—I can't find it, Thomas said.

—What? Jon said.

—The Big Dipper.

—Does it matter?

—Yes.

Thomas leaned forward and took the wine bottle from Jon's hand.

—Have a little wine, Jon said.

Jon looked at the surf and Thomas leaned his head back.

They sat like that for a while.

—All the big things, Thomas said suddenly. For some reason, we can only approach them in images.

—What?

—Take the stars, for example. We can't see them the way they are, we arrange them into constellations. It's the same with death, or having a child. What can you say about it? But if you can find the right imagery.

—Yeah.

—Life is great, Thomas said.

—Maybe I'm not drunk enough.

—C'mon, stop whining.

Thomas handed him the bottle. Jon leaned his head back and looked for the Big Dipper as he drank.

—I can see two, he said. He pointed with the bottle. A small one up here and a bigger one there.

—No way, Thomas said.

Jon pointed again.

—God damn, you're right.

Thomas glanced from one to the other.

—Maybe we should go inside and wake up the others. Tell them we've made an astronomical discovery.

—I think Charlotte wants to sleep, Jon said.

—Isn't Vivian just fucking beautiful.

—Yeah, Jon said. She's pretty amazing. You're really lucky.

—Everything's just a matter of luck. It's all chance.

—Yes, Jon said.

—Charlotte is beautiful too. She's a really nice girl.

Thomas stood and pulled his T-shirt over his head.

—C'mon, he said. Let's go swimming.

He unzipped his pants and pulled them down all the way to his shoes. Then he sat down on the boat and untied his laces. A moment later he stood naked before Jon.

—Don't you think it's too cold?

—Not at all. It's never been warmer.

—And don't you think you're too drunk?

—Hell no.

Thomas turned and ran toward the sea. Jon could see Thomas' body standing out white against the dark water. Thomas ran until the darkness reached his knees. A ways out, the water was shallow. A splash. After that Jon saw Thomas in glimpses, a foot, a white arm, the upper part of his back. Then there was only the sound left, the rhythmic strokes and now and then a splash from his feet. Then even the sounds fell silent, drowned out by the beating of the waves and by Jon's own breathing.

A moment later Jon got up and walked down to the water. Rocks and shells bit into his feet. He stared into the darkness. The moon gave the sea a thin, flickering sheen of light. Below the surface the water was dark, and seemed darker than usual because the lights played tricks with his eyes.

Some time passed.

Then he called out,

—Thomas.

—Thomas! he called out even louder.

—Thomas, he called out a third time.

All the way out by the third sandbank, an arm appeared.

—C'mon! There's...The wind carried the last part of the sentence away.

—What? Jon shouted.

—Come on out here. There's phosphor.

Jon pulled off his jeans. He shrugged off his white T-shirt, then his underwear. They landed on top of the pile a few feet from the water.

The water was surprisingly warm, even a bit warmer than the air. Jon saw a swarm of small, glowing particles at his feet; he bent down, and scooped up a handful of water, letting it fall. The phosphor flashed briefly, then fell into the darkness. He squatted down and drove his hand through the water; it took on a green sheen and looked bigger. He pulled it up and then put it back in again. Then he stood, took a couple steps, and began to run. He ran until he couldn't anymore, and then let himself fall headfirst into the water, dived and crawled with long, calm strokes. For each stroke he turned his head, taking in air from the left and breathing out to the right.

On the second sandbank the water was too shallow for him to swim, and he got up and walked a few steps. He looked out towards the third sandbank but couldn't see his brother. He hurled himself forward.

When he reached the last sandbank he let his feet sink down, and glanced around. Thomas was nowhere in sight. Jon spun around, ran an arm through the water, and swirled the phosphor. Just then, he felt something grab hold of his right foot. He fell backwards and felt the water gush up his nose and into his sinuses. A moment later he got back on his feet. He threw himself at Thomas and tried to dunk his head under the water. Thomas got away from him and shoved a handful of water in his face. Jon threw himself forward again and this time he managed to grab Thomas's hair with both hands. He pressed Thomas's head under water and held it there a few seconds.

—Truce? he said, as he pulled Thomas back up.

—Truce, Thomas said, laughing.

Jon let him go and Thomas splashed him again.

—Stop it.

—What's wrong with you? Thomas said, pressing his hands together and shoving saltwater against Jon.

Jon leapt forward and swam away underwater. He had barely emerged when Thomas was on him again.

Jon took two steps away from Thomas, then turned and smacked him across the cheek. Thomas grabbed his hand before he managed to pull it away. They stood motionless across from each other.

—Look at me, Thomas said.

—Sorry, Jon said.

—Look at me, Thomas said.

—It's not enough that I say I'm sorry?

—No.

Jon looked at him.

—Now tell me what's wrong?

Jon exhaled and stared up at the stars. He glanced toward Thomas, fastening his gaze at a point just above his eyes.

—I don't know.

—You don't know?

—Maybe I shouldn't have come.

—Why?

—I don't know. I just shouldn't have come.

Thomas still had a solid grip on Jon's wrist. They stood opposite each other, the water reaching their chests. The water was dark and still, and the phosphorescence had subsided. They stood without speaking for almost a minute.

—Don't you ever miss him? Jon finally said.

—Who?

—Who do you think?

Thomas let go of Jon's hand.

—Of course I miss him, he said.

—I can't help thinking of him now that we're here.

—Why?

—I don't know. Maybe because it was here he was happiest. That's what everyone says.

—Of course I think about him, Thomas said. But not all the time. It comes and goes.

Jon drew a hand through the water and the phosphor sparkled.

—I'm freezing, Thomas said. Let's swim back.

They swam slowly toward the beach, side by side with three or four feet between them.

Jon took a few powerful strokes, then let himself sink under the water. He squeezed his eyes shut to keep the water out. He lay against the bottom, sand scraping against his chest. Soon after he surfaced for air.

Thomas had stood and waded through the shallow water a few steps ahead. Jon followed.

They hadn't brought any towels. They grabbed their clothes and ran toward the house. The sand on the path was cool on their feet, and there was a smell of heather and resin in the air. They sprinted across the yard.

The towels hung on a clothesline drawn between two birch trees. They dried quickly, and pulled on their underwear and T-Shirts.

Before Jon opened the door to the house, he glanced at Thomas.

—Look, I'm sorry…

—It's all right, Thomas said. No need to apologize.

—We're going home tomorrow, Charlotte and I.

—Okay.

Jon opened the door and walked into the low-ceilinged living room.

—Sleep well, he said, before they parted.

Jon crawled into bed beside Charlotte. She turned in her sleep and clutched his thumb. He arranged his duvet and blanket with his free hand, and gradually he warmed up. From the bed he could make out the photograph of his father, which was hanging on the wall. The photo, set in a thin silver frame, had been taken down by the beach. He was wearing an Icelandic sweater and was looking directly at the camera. Before long Jon heard the bed squeal in the room next to his; then he heard a low, rhythmic moan. He couldn't decide if it was coming from Vivian or his brother. After a while he realized it was coming from Vivian.

Chairs

Martha woke early. She sat up halfway in bed and gazed through the darkness. She could make out the television and the writing desk on the other side of the room, and then she knew where she was.

She set her feet on the floor and went into the kitchen. She washed herself at the sink and started the coffee. She stepped out into the cold hall, opened her dresser, and found a blouse and a skirt.

When the coffee was ready, she sat at the table in the living room. She glanced at the bed; it was hard to get used to it standing right there. She looked out the window, and could just make out the bare branches on the tree outside.

She drank her coffee and warmed her hands on the cup. Slowly the tree emerged from the darkness. She saw the rough bark at the base of the trunk, and she could see how the trunk split into thinner and thinner branches. Those at the top weren't any thicker than a finger.

She thought about a book she'd once given Isak. *To Draw is to See*, it was called. She remembered that he'd drawn the tree. He'd also tried to draw her hands. That was the hardest, he'd said. He himself had had large, blocky hands with raised blue veins; the pencil had looked small between his thick fingers.

Martha rose and searched the bookshelf. She studied the brittle spines carefully, but she didn't find the book. Then she heard the mail slot click and she went out to the entryway.

She picked up her newspaper and headed back to her chair at the window.

After she'd read the newspaper, she walked through the kitchen and out to the hall. She opened the lid on the commode, but closed it again immediately. Instead she went to the stairwell. She clutched the banister and moved slowly up the stairs. She rested in the chair on the landing, but felt neither dizzy nor out of breath. She continued up, and soon she was able to sit down on the cold toilet seat and urinate in peace.

When she'd washed her hands, she moved across the hall to Thorkild's room. She opened the brown, glass-fronted bookcase and began searching. The books were covered with a thin layer of yellowed dust, and many had no spine; they'd been read and reread by children and grandchildren; she pulled the books out so she could read the titles on the first page. She was reminded of how Isak had sat on the porch with *The Postman Always Rings Twice*, *The Woman in the Lake*, or *They Shoot Horses, Don't They?* She grabbed the threadbare copy of *Postman* and began reading. She read the first page standing up, then she sat on the chair at the side of the bed. She read about Frank and Cora and their strange passion, and though she was repulsed by the violence, warmth rippled through her body.

Frank and Cora had just rid themselves of her husband when Martha heard the key in the door. She felt a little lightheaded.

—Mrs. Jakobsen, your lunch.

—Thank you, she replied. Be a dear and set it on the table.

—Where are you?

Martha stood and moved to the top of the stairs.

—Here.

—Let me give you a hand.

John placed the aluminum tray on her bureau. Before she could protest, he was on his way up the stairs. He was a rather large, ruddy man, and Martha felt a little uncomfortable in his presence. He followed her down the stairs all the way to the dining table in the living room, and then he retrieved her meal.

With a smile and an almost tender "Goodbye, Mrs. Jakobsen," he left. Martha shook her head. She stood and went into the kitchen to get a plate and silverware.

After lunch, Martha climbed the stairs again, this time with a longer rest on the way. She picked up the book and thumbed through it from the back to the front. The edges were nearly yellow, dog-eared, with a few brown spots she couldn't identify. On the title page something caught her attention. It appeared there'd been a dedication at one time. The paper was a little more delicate, in some places almost transparent. She held the page up toward the light; she could just read a few words: "My beloved," "Soon," "Karen." It was her sister's handwriting. Martha examined the other side. The book was published in 1934, two years after she and Isak were married. She sat down.

She remembered her sister's red-eyed, almost aggressive condolences following Isak's death. And before: how she became nervous whenever he stepped into the room. She remembered the softness in Isak's voice when he said: "Karen, so nice to see you." And first and foremost, she remembered the summer Thorkild was born, how Karen kept her house while she was at the hospital. Martha squeezed the book between her hands. On the dust jacket, she read how this was a story about "impossible love, burning desire, and unavoidable destruction." Was there a reason she'd never felt the urge to read it? She'd outlived both of them, but their secret had almost survived her.

After a while, she stood, closed the rattling glass door of the bookcase, and began her backwards descent down the stairs with one hand on the banister, the other on the book. She rested at the landing. That's the way it is, growing old, she thought: one moves from chair to chair.

She sat at her writing desk with her back to the window, and there she spent most of the afternoon. The darkness drained through the window on the opposite wall and turned the sofa, dining table, bookshelf, and bed into nothing but points and lines around her. Finally, she switched on the table lamp.

She opened the book and began reading. She read about the court case and how Frank and Cora were acquitted; about Kennedy, who tried to blackmail them; and then about the accident in which Cora was killed. When she read the ending, where Frank was found guilty of Cora's murder, she had no doubts: it was unjust. Frank would never do such a thing.

Then she closed the book and looked around the room. Outside it was completely dark, and the curtains needed to be drawn. No, she thought as she rose from the chair, I'm not jealous. Then she turned and drew the curtains closed. She headed for the window on the other side of the room.

Milk

had just lit a cigarette. The flame didn't really take, so I pursed my lips and puffed. As I puffed, I happened to emit a small whistle. Wanting to hide that it was by accident, I added a few notes. It was the beginning of a theme, I repeated the notes a few times, and suddenly the rest came by itself. I couldn't quite remember which piece it was. The melody grooved back and forth across my lips. There was *pizzazz* in it, the kind that could put you in a good mood. I let the cigarette smoke itself and whistled away.

I was standing beside the window and suddenly felt the need to take a walk. It was gray and windy outside, and I had no errands to make, but I felt such an urge to get out. I turned to Emma sitting at the dining table reading a magazine.

—I think I'll go for a walk.

She glanced up quickly, then down again.

—It's raining, she said.

—I know, I said.

—You'll get wet, she said.

—Yeah, I said.

I'd stopped whistling, but the melody hung on the edge of my lips.

—What's wrong, Olaf? You'll get sick if you go out, you know that.

I turned back to the window.

—Yeah, I said.

had my coat on, ready to go, when Emma stepped into the hallway.

—You'll catch pneumonia, she said.

—Give it up, I responded with a sharpness in my voice that surprised us both.

waited a bit for the elevator. As it crawled up from the first floor, I could see the numbers light up one by one. It made a rusty clang, and the doors opened. I stepped on and pushed L, but the elevator continued upwards. At the 12th floor it came to a stop, and a short, fat man stepped on. He smelled ripe, of body odor and beer. I've not grown handsomer with age—I'll admit as much—but I maintain a certain level of hygiene. I could see that my disgust was reciprocated; he was just as annoyed as I was at having to share the cramped space. As the elevator lowered us down the shaft, we didn't exchange a single word. About halfway down I thought of my theme. I hummed it carefully, and after a few irritated sideways glances from my companion, I began to whistle. He shifted his weight from one leg to the other and cleared his throat, and I simply whistled louder. Six floors down the doors opened, and we got off. The little man hurried away.

Outside, rain fell lightly. The cars in the lot were gleaming, their colors clean and sharp. Large puddles of water lay on the lot; here and there were grates in the curb, and I could hear the water gurgling beneath my feet. The weather was good for a walk, the risk of meeting someone minimal; for someone my age the risk is minimal to begin with, but in this kind of weather it's as good as zero. I followed the sidewalk along the parking lot, past the neighboring block, past the playground, and past the supermarket with the red signs.

I'd reached the last block when the rain started coming down hard. I walked along a narrow drainage ditch; there was a bank on the other side of the ditch, and on the other side of the bank was the freeway. Through the rain, I could just hear the cars whizzing past. The path I walked on was muddy, and I moved forward in short steps and with my vision focused on the ground. The rain made my neck and back cold. When I stopped to orient myself, I discovered something strange. The water in the ditch had changed color. It had a white sheen. At first I thought it was because of the stream, but as I continued along the path, I noticed how the water became increasingly murky.

After I'd walked around 300 feet, I came to a pipe poking out of the bank. The white liquid was spewing here; the liquid running from the pipe resembled undiluted paint. I managed to squat down and put a finger in the water. I held it up to my nose, and because I couldn't smell anything, I tasted it cautiously. It was milk. I bent forward and put my hand under the pipe, pulled it out, and drank. I don't usually drink milk, not since I was a child have I done so—not even in my coffee—but it tasted fresh and good. I stood and continued walking. My knees ached, but I ignored the pain. I didn't feel like going home.

The noise grew progressively louder the farther up I went. I climbed the broad steps one at a time, making short pauses along the way. The railing was slick with rain, but it was better than no support. I reached the top and moved out along the narrow bridge. There was no one here, no one except me. From here, I had a complete view of the freeway. A number of emergency vehicles were parked there: two rescue vehicles, three ambulances, and a police car. Lying across both lanes was a sixty-foot tanker truck. Its oval, steel tank was leaking in several places, and milk was gushing out. A smaller car had driven into the overturned tanker, and two rescue workers were cutting passengers out of the car. A passenger of a third vehicle was quickly covered with a blanket and rushed to an ambulance.

I had only stood there a few minutes when I heard footsteps from the other end of the bridge. My mood grew no less hostile when I saw who it was. It was my brother Albert. I cursed at myself: I should know better, I thought, Albert has always had a nose for accidents. I looked away, stiffly ignoring him when he came over and stood right beside me.

Down on the freeway, the rescue team had taken a few steps back with their cutting torches, and the ambulance crew began lifting the driver from the vehicle. I saw a woman lifted out and put on a stretcher. There was not a drop of blood anywhere; her clothes were coated with a dull, wet film. Her face and hair were white as a sheet or a statue. I started whistling. It soothed me. I could tell that it made Albert uncomfortable, but that didn't stop me from doing it. I whistled the same theme as before, a splendid piece, it gave me air, gave me an unaccustomed strength, an unaccustomed feeling of freedom. Meanwhile, I stared at the milk gushing out onto the road, and at the rescue workers who now stood smoking, their welder's goggles pushed up on their foreheads, wet, completely soaked with milk and rain.

—I know that piece, Albert said suddenly. It's Mozart.

I immediately stopped whistling.

—No, I said.

Albert waited for me to be more specific, but I had nothing more to say. It was apparently impossible to keep anything for yourself in this world.

Then he changed the subject:

—It doesn't look good, eh.

The last of the ambulances drove off under a sky of gloomy, blue-black clouds.

—But they're in God's hands, he continued. That's a consolation.

—Do you still believe in that crap?

The words rushed from me.

—Yes, Olaf, I do. Even you are in God's hands, whether you want to be or not.

I stared out over at the freeway and tried to control myself.

—Tell me, he went on calmly. Don't you hope for a life after this?

The water dripped from my nose like a tap. My coat was heavy with rain, but I barely felt it.

—No, I said. I'm hoping for a place to be alone. A grave, for example.

Albert put a hand on my shoulder.

—You're all too proud, Olaf, that's no good.

I removed his hand from my shoulder.

—You don't know me, I said.

Then I walked away.

Fling

They drove in silence. Martin glanced at Anne, who looked out the window at the countryside. Her hair was a little blonder at the tips, she was suntanned, and he could see light traces of salt on her skin. Close by the fields flitted past, farther away they formed patterns of yellow and green. He gazed at the car's clock and then at the road again.

They were driving back to the city.

Martin slowed down and signaled for a left turn.

—There's something I'd like to show you, he said.

They turned onto a narrow country road that led between hills. Martin smiled and stared at the road, Anne looked at Martin, then at the clock.

The rye-covered hills rose up on both sides and forced the road into large, winding turns. Anne put a hand on the back of Martin's seat then let it drift up his neck and into his hair, which was stiff from the salt.

After a few miles the hills disappeared from the road, and a flat area of fields and small orchards spread out before them. They drove over a creek, past a cornfield, past a pine farm.

—This is it, Martin said.

He turned left down a narrow gravel road. The grass was high between the tracks and brushed the car's undercarriage.

They coasted into the driveway and parked next to an old truck with fruit crates stacked on the trailer bed. On the right was a whitewashed farmhouse, to the left a shed with a rusted pipe sticking up from the roof.

Martin and Anne got out of the car. The air smelled of apples and smoked fish.

—We used to come here quite often when I was a kid, Martin said.

He went up to the farmhouse.

—Let's see if anyone's here.

At the side of the house there was a little garden and behind that an orchard. The grass was tall and green, even though it was late summer.

Anne remained standing in the middle of the driveway.

Martin knocked on the door, which had a square window shaped like a diamond. He peered in, but the room behind the door lay in darkness. He waited a moment, then returned to Anne.

—Let's look over here, he said.

Martin walked towards the shed. The door was ajar, and he looked in. Long rows of trout hung under the ceiling. The walls of the little room were smeared black, and the light from the door opening didn't reach the back wall. The fish gleamed with oil, the skins golden and brown, the fins almost black.

—Have a look. This is where they smoke them.

Anne came over and stood next to Martin. She put her arm around his waist.

—That's trout, he said.

—Is it?

—I hope somebody's here. Maybe they're in the back.

Martin turned and worked himself free of her arm.

They walked down a short path that began to the right of the shed. The ground was damp, and there were nettles on either side.

At the end of the path were the fishponds, five of them constructed in rows with several feet of grass between each. Martin and Anne could see all the way down to the end.

They moved to the edge of the first pond and looked into the water. The surface was calm, mirroring the sky's moving clouds;

it was only after their eyes had adjusted to the light that they could see down into the dark water. The fish stood still. Once in a while there was one that moved, and the silver-colored fins and white belly shot a spark of sunlight back up through the dark-green water.

—Trout, Martin said. Let's see what's in the next one.

Anne stayed where she was and looked down into the water.

—Martin, she said.

—Yeah?

—Let's go. I don't like this place.

—Hold on a minute.

Martin walked to the edge of the next pond. Here the fish were packed in tighter. He strained his eyes to see the bottom, but he couldn't.

Then he went back to Anne.

—That was trout too, he said.

—I don't know what it is, she said. I think it's too quiet here.

—That's all right, he said.

They walked back along the path, and this time she walked ahead of him. Martin snapped off a long blade of grass and tickled her arm with it just above the elbow. Anne drew her arm back. He tickled her again, and again she moved her arm away. Then he tossed the grass down.

They came out on the driveway and walked over to the car. Anne stopped suddenly. There was something on the hood of the car: a plum, a fat purple plum. Martin walked over. He picked up the plum and looked around. There were no trees nearby. The door to the farmhouse was closed, and the door to the smokehouse stood half-open, as before.

—Come on, Anne said. Let's go.

Martin set the plum on the truck's running board and unlocked the car. They sat down and closed the doors.

—Must've been some kids, Martin said.

They drove back along the gravel driveway and then onto the asphalt road. They drove past the pine farm, past the cornfield, and over the creek and in between the hills. Finally they were on the main road.

—Martin, Anne said, after they'd driven for a little while.

—Yeah?

—I don't think I can keep this up much longer. We've got to do something soon. We've got to make a decision.

—Yeah, Martin said.

He looked at the dashboard clock and then again at the oncoming road. A moment later he turned and looked at Anne.

—Yeah, he said.

Albatross

My brother sat on the couch reading a magazine. I aimed at him with my lighter pistol and pulled the trigger. The flame rose straight up, almost five inches high, but he didn't react.

—Catch!

I tossed the lighter at him over the coffee table. He dropped the magazine and threw himself toward the lighter in order to save the couch and curtains and wall-to-wall carpet. He couldn't find it and started pulling the pillows down on the floor.

—Jeppe, you dick. Where'd it go? You'll burn the house down.

The lighter lay on the floor right at his feet. I stood and walked over. The flame had gone out as soon as I'd let go.

—Here, I said and handed it to him.

—You're an idiot, he said, refusing the lighter.

I stuffed the lighter in my pocket and left the room. I put on my boots and jacket and walked through the empty stalls and out the other side. We'd not been outdoors for two days. The afternoon sky was clear and blue, and I tromped toward our neighbor's place. Svend the Hen was scorching his field; he'd lit rows of straw on the opposite side, and the fire now ran in parallel tracks over the crest of a hill. He was busy plowing a security barrier so the fire wouldn't leap over onto our field, which hadn't been harvested yet. He brought the tractor to a halt and opened the cab door.

—Get in.

I grabbed the handrail inside the door and hoisted myself up. Svend the Hen had his shotgun across his thigh, the barrel snapped open and draped over his leg. I sat on the wheel guard, and the tractor started with a jerk. Svend the Hen's short silver hair poked out of the corner of a green cap. He didn't say anything. He plowed another row along the barrier to our field.

—So, he said.

I could see how the effort of talking stretched his cheeks, how his lips twitched in the attempt, and how he sat chewing on what he would say. As if he had to put his tongue and lips in order first. As we reached the end of the row, he turned the tractor and began a third row.

—So...They're on vacation or what?

—Yeah, I said.

—What about the other hen?

—He's at home.

—Well, well, then.

He always called us hens—maybe because he didn't have any kids of his own. Some said he fucked his cows, but I had never believed it.

—Well then, he said again after a minute.

He smiled for an instant. Not because he liked to, but more because he couldn't help himself, I think. Or maybe because he was proud that he'd managed to get his tongue in the right position in his mouth, moved his lips and all that. His teeth didn't look too good, and you couldn't mistake the smell. Maybe everything's going rotten in there, I thought. He turned the tractor up near the shrubbery and drove with the plow raised in the direction of the fire. He took two bullets from a box on the front window and stuck them in the shotgun, still with one hand on the steering wheel. As we reached the first burning column, he turned the tractor so we were driving along the front. He opened the door and asked me to steer. The air was heavy with black dust, and it was hot as hell. We'd almost reached the end of the field before anything happened. He aimed and fired in almost the same instant. I barely registered what had happened.

—God damn, he mumbled.

I saw a hare leaping away.

—God damn, I said.

At that moment I saw another hare. Svend the Hen fired and this time he got it. The hare rolled a somersault, then lay completely still. He stopped the tractor and opened the door on my side, and with a nod of the head let me know what he wanted me to do. I hopped down and ran over to pick up the hare. I grabbed its legs and swung it around high over my head. The flames came closer; it was a wall of heat moving in my direction. I ran back to the tractor and tossed the hare to him.

—Get in, he said.

I shook my head.

—I gotta go, I said.

He closed the door, touched his fingers to his cap, and a moment later he was off in a cloud of black smoke.

I looked around for a place where I could get through the fire. I found an opening then made a running start and leaped through. When I came out on the other side, my face felt stiff and my hair smelled charred.

The ground was black and scorched.

At the end of the field, I found a smoldering chunk of a tree. It was a branch from an oak that stood near the border of our land. I picked up the cold end and went toward our side. Near the track separating the two fields, I stopped and looked around. The rye should've been harvested a long time ago; in many places the stalks lay horizontal to the ground. Ours was the only field, as far as I could see, that didn't have stubble, or wasn't already plowed up. I stood there a moment considering the pros and cons. They can kiss my ass, I thought. Then I threw the branch as far as I could into the field.

I hiked across Svend the Hen's field. I headed down through the bog, followed the railroad tracks a short distance, and then walked through a small stand of spruce.

I'd reached the main road when I heard the first fire truck. It drove toward me at high speed, and a moment later the second one followed. I could see the firemen putting on their gear. I tramped along the road meeting one car after another—curiosity-seekers following the fire trucks, I think. I also saw someone on a bicycle. I could hear the sirens approaching from every direction.

Along the way I passed a large white farm, and I saw a man and a woman hastily getting their children inside a car. After a few hundred feet, I passed a Dutch barn stuffed with hay, and half a mile later came to a wide field of barley that hadn't been harvested.

Before long, I could see the first houses in what passed for the area's biggest town. Towering up over all the houses was a grain silo. And I could see the brownstone school building with its white windows.

Just as I got to town, the local cop drove toward me in his blue Volvo. I waved at him and he waved back, and then he was already long past me.

I crossed the road, and soon stood in front of a broad chain-link gate. Three trucks were parked in the lot, but there was nobody around. I clambered over the gate and walked toward the silo. Small piles of grain lay here and there, and the smell was sweet and good. I put my hand on the outer wall; it felt warm. I went around the silo and found a door behind the building. With a hard jerk, I got the door open and went inside. I stood in a pretty narrow shaft; on the wall were a number of shiny steel stairs, and far above, I noticed a small circle of blue light, which I guessed was the sky.

I started crawling. It was really hot inside the shaft, and when I reached the halfway point, I had to stop and take my jacket off. I tied it around my waist, but that only made crawling more difficult, so I let it fall. I continued up; the higher I got, the warmer it was.

When I finally crawled onto the roof, I was soaked through with sweat. I pulled my shirt over my head and looked toward the south. I could see a huge black cloud of smoke; under it, an orange glow. I couldn't see the flames. In the foreground, I could see a combine that'd now begun to harvest the field I'd just passed.

I looked at the parking lot below; the three trucks were slightly staggered and resembled toys on display. The houses in the town were unusually close, but they still seemed small. Patio furniture filled the square yards, but there were no people. Furthest away was the train station, and I could see the red train waiting for the regional train.

I turned toward the north and saw a blue glare, which I knew was the sea. Then I turned toward the south and looked at the red glow.

Soon after, I sat down. I flicked my lighter and watched the flame. I fell into a trance and sat that way for a long time. At some point I realized I was freezing. I stood and put on my shirt, but it was cold and damp. I stared toward the south: As far as I could see the flames were burning out.

I moved to the hatch and started crawling back down.

I headed back the same way I'd come. Outside the town limits, I passed the cop. I waved, and he waved back politely. I passed the barley field and greeted the farmhand, who leaned up against the grain wagon smoking. I passed the Dutch barn where two boys shot at a target with a bow. There were lights in the stalls at the big farm, and I could hear the sound of a transistor radio through the open door.

I followed the main road and walked through the little stand of spruce, followed the railroad tracks, and walked through the bog.

It had grown dark by the time I finally made it home. At a distance I could see the light in the living room. I shuffled forward through a thick layer of gray ash. The fire had burned up most of the field; it hadn't been brought under control until about 150 feet from the house.

When I walked inside, my brother sat on the couch watching television. He looked up.

—Where have you been? he said. There was a fire in the fields.

—I know that, I said.

I looked at the screen. I could see a big white bird lying on a nest: an albatross.

—There were a lot of people here. The cop was here, too. He was over talking to Svend the Hen. He seemed to think it was his fault.

I walked into the kitchen and poured a bowl of cornflakes. When I got back, my brother had changed the channel to some kind of quiz show; from a few notes you were supposed to guess the name of a song or a piece of music. I sat down in the seat opposite him.

They played a few bars of a song.

—"Strangers in the Night"! my brother called out.

We waited for the answer.

—You see, he said.

I pulled the lighter from my pocket, and this time I didn't flick it—I just tossed it over to him.

—Catch! I said.

He flicked it and saw that the flame was only an inch high. He looked at me and then set it down on the coffee table.

—They say he fucks his cows.

—Yeah, I said and watched the screen.

They played a few bars of a new tune.

—Can't we watch the show with the albatrosses? I said.

—Okay.

For a long time, without saying a word, we watched the program about the enormous birds. The narrator said they could fly up to a 600 miles a day. They sailed on the wind almost without moving their wings. We saw how they dived after fish, and we saw an albatross egg that was the size of a honey melon.

At some point, my brother turned his head and looked at me. I didn't look at him, but I could feel his gaze; he watched me for a pretty long time. Then he turned his attention back to the screen.

—Promise you'll never do that again, he said under his breath.

Acknowledgments

The author and translator would like to thank the following journals where these stories, sometimes in slightly altered format, first appeared:

"What is it?" and "Fling" (as "Summer") in *Redivider*, Volume 6, No. 2

"Tide" in *The Brooklyn Review*, 25

"Unsettled" in *The Bitter Oleander*, Volume 14, No. 2

"Phosphorescence" in *A River & Sound Review*

"Kramer" in *Copper Nickel*, 14

"Hair" in *World Literature Today*, September/October 2010

"Rose" and "Crossing" in *Portland Review*, Issue 56, Volume 3

"Intercom" (as "Markus") in *Absinthe: New European Fiction*, Winter 2011

"Albatross" in *Numéro Cinq*

Photo by Camilla Hultén Fruelund

About Simon Fruelund

The Danish author Simon Fruelund has written six books, among them *Borgerligt tusmørke* (2006)—published as *Civil Twilight* by Spout Hill Press in 2013 and *Verden og Varvara* (The World and Varvara, 2009). His latest book is *Pendlerne* (The Commuters, 2014). His work has been translated into Italian, Swedish, and English, and his short stories have appeared in a number of magazines across the U.S., including *World Literature Today, The Collagist, Redivider,* and *Absinthe: New European Fiction.* Find him on the web at simonfruelund.com.

Photo by Eric Druxman

About the translator

K.E. Semmel's work has appeared in *Ontario Review, Washington Post, World Literature Today,* and elsewhere. He has translated 11 books from Norwegian and Danish and is a recipient of numerous grants from the Danish Arts Foundation. A 2016 NEA Literary Translation Fellow, he lives in Rochester, NY. Find him online: kesemmel.com.

Also from Santa Fe Writers Project

Wars of Heaven *by Richard Currey*

A powerful, tender collection of stories about the working class in West Virginia at the turn of the last century.

> *"A beautiful book...a lasting contribution to American literature."*
> — John Sutherland, Seattle Times

The Poor Children *by April L. Ford*

Ford explores the eccentric, the perverse, the disenfranchised, and the darkly comic possibilities at play win us all.

> *"From the amazing first sentence of April L. Ford's debut collection, The Poor Children, I was hooked. This is a rarity: a compellingly original voice and vision."*
> — David Morrell,
> New York Times *bestselling author*

The Fires *by Alan Cheuse*

Two linked novellas portray finely-honed portraits of hope and change in which some characters succeed and others fail on separate but equally compelling quests.

> *"Startlingly beautiful stories in their searing radiance and molten heat."*
> — Booklist

About Santa Fe Writers Project

SFWP is an independent press founded in 1998 that embraces a mission of artistic preservation, recognizing exciting new authors, and bringing out of print work back to the shelves.

Find us on Facebook, Twitter @sfwp, and at www.sfwp.com *s*f**WP**)